This book belongs to

....

Topaz

The Sunken Treasure

Topaz

The Sunken Treasure

Rose Lacey

Willow
Tree

Published by Willow Tree Books, 2018
Willow Tree Books, Tide Mill Way, Woodbridge, Suffolk, IP12 1AP

0 2 4 6 8 9 7 5 3 1

Series concept © 2018 Willow Tree Books
Text © 2018 Working Partners Limited
London, WC1X 9HH
Cover illustration © 2018 Willow Tree Books
Interior illustrations © 2018 Willow Tree Books

Special thanks to Lil Chase

Willow Tree Books, Princess Pirates and associated logos are
trademarks and/or registered trademarks of Tide Mill Media Ltd

ISBN: 978-1-78700-456-6
Printed and bound in Great Britain
by Bell and Bain Ltd, Glasgow

www.willowtreebooks.net

For Hayley Kark,
my number 1 crew member

Prologue

It would be remembered as the kingdoms' darkest day.

The five royal families of Lemuria stood on the ship's deck as destruction rained down around them. Cannons boomed, fires burned, the islands they had once ruled were reduced to rubble.

It was the day that I—Celestine, the seawitch—had hoped would never come: Obsidian, in all her wickedness, had defeated us.

Each king and queen wept as they placed

their babies in baskets, as I instructed. Parting
with their beloved girls was the only way to keep
the princesses safe. Each queen removed a ring
from her finger and hid it within the folds of her
baby's blanket.

Obsidian might rule, but without the five
magical Treasures of Lemuria she'd have no real
power. And without the rings, she'd be unable to
discover where those Treasures were hidden. She
hadn't won. Not yet.

As the babies were lowered from the ship
into the waves, I cast my spell. Instantly, a circle
of calm water and still air surrounded them.

"The sea will take them somewhere safe,"
I told their sobbing parents. "Somewhere far
away from here."

We watched as the five beautiful infants
drifted away.

Then came a huge explosion as a final

cannonball hit the ship. We'd saved the babies, but no magic I possessed could save their parents. The ship and everyone on it sunk to the bottom of the ocean.

Though the kings and queens were lost, one day the ship would rise and sail again. And those young princesses would return and restore this world to the peaceful place it once was.

The saviors of Lemuria.

***

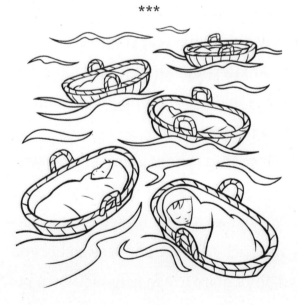

Chapter 1

The two boats in front of them were neck and neck. Topaz could already see the yellow buoys that marked the finish line bobbing in the water ahead, and knew that their little sailing boat would have to do something major if they were going to win today.

The best thing about going to Breakwater Hall boarding school was that it stood beside Lapis Lake. The lake was surrounded by woodland paths and rocky slopes, and was so big you needed binoculars to see across it. On a perfect

day like this, in early fall, when the sun was warm and the wind blew, there was nothing Topaz liked more than being out on the water with her best friends. Most pupils at Breakwater Hall took sailing as a subject, and every month all the crews were invited to race around Lapis Lake.

Topaz was the oldest of their crew, and the captain—it was up to her to find a way to overtake the two leading boats. Squeezing between the two boats would be risky, but quicker than trying to go around them. The four-girl crew would have to move fast to avoid a crash. She pushed back her heavy locks of auburn hair and turned to her crew. "Go between them!" she shouted over the noise of the rushing air.

"Huh?" Pearl replied, tilting her head questioningly.

"Tighten the jib sheet!" Topaz shouted back.

But Pearl grabbed the wrong rope!

The heavy boom at the bottom of the sail swung across the little boat. Coral was looking in the other direction, but luckily Opal had seen it. She pushed Coral out of the way just in time. Coral landed sprawled on the plastic bottom of the boat. On the shore, the crowd of watching girls and teachers gasped.

There was no way they could pass between the boats without colliding. Topaz had made a big mistake!

"Slacken off!" Topaz shouted. The other girls let the sails out and the boat slowed. Topaz forced the tiller over, turning the boat to the right. An oncoming crew swept past. *Oh no,* thought Topaz. *We're even further behind!*

"Boat Nestor—fourth place!" their headmistress, Miss Whitestone, called through her megaphone as they passed the finish line.

Topaz clenched her fists in frustration.

Water splashed Opal's dark skin as she leaned over and stroked the black stallion's head painted on the side of their boat. "Bad luck, Nestor," she said. Opal talked to Nestor after every race and it always made Topaz smile.

"Never mind," said Pearl, springing up from where she was sitting. "We'll get them next time. Come on girls, ring bump!"

The four friends brought their right fists forward. They all had similar rings—gold bands with a single stone, each one a different color and shape. It was a weird coincidence—how had four orphans with matching rings all ended up at the same school? The friends had wondered about it many times...but they had never come up with a good answer.

"All friends on deck!" they said, touching their rings together.

After taking Nestor back to the dock and neatly stowing everything away, they headed inside. Breakwater Hall looked more like a royal palace than a school—battlements at the front, stained-glass windows, and even turrets with pointed roofs. Topaz had lived here for as long as she could remember—the school was her home —but its ancient beauty never failed to take her breath away.

Coral took off her life vest and ran her fingers through her thick red hair. "I love sailing," she said, pulling out a comb and tackling the knots, "But I hate what it does to my hair!"

Pearl grinned, her pink cheeks even rosier than normal because of the sun. "If we had a penny for every time you said that, we could hire you a personal makeover artist."

Coral's eyes opened wide. "I would love that!"

They all giggled, but Topaz still felt bad.

"You're blaming yourself, aren't you?" asked Opal, falling into step beside her as they walked through the corridors and up a sweeping staircase to the dorms.

Topaz frowned. "Am I that obvious?"

Opal nodded. "Yup. And you know you shouldn't. A captain is only as good as their team."

"That's just it," Topaz said, grabbing Opal's hand and giving it a squeeze. "With you three, I have the best team ever!" she sighed. "So why can't we win?"

"We will," said Opal, "we just—"

"Huh?!" Pearl had pushed open the door to their shared dorm. She stopped in the doorway, staring in.

Topaz caught up. Their dorm was a circular room built into one of the turrets, with three windows looking out over the majestic lake below. Each girl had a bed, a desk, and a closet for their clothes. But today there were five of everything instead of four.

"What in the oceans...?" said Opal, peering over Topaz's shoulder.

It was obvious to Topaz; they were getting a new roommate. She felt a stab of unease. The four friends shared a room because they were the only girls who lived here all year, with no homes to go to during the holidays. Bringing in a new girl would feel very strange.

"Why would Miss Whitestone–?" Topaz wondered aloud.

And as if by magic, Miss Whitestone appeared. "Knock knock," she said, tapping on the door frame. "Can we come in?"

Standing beside Miss Whitestone was a pretty girl with straight black hair in a long braid and deep green oval eyes.

"Girls, this is Jade," said Miss Whitestone.

Jade looked at the floor, blinking nervously.

Miss Whitestone gestured for Jade to go into the room. "She's going to be your new roommate," she finished.

"Hi," said Coral.

"Welcome," said Topaz, smiling warmly.

Jade still couldn't meet their eyes. Topaz watched her carefully. *What was her story? Why was she starting late in the semester? Would she be friendly?*

"Why is she in *our* room?" Pearl blurted.

"Pearl!" the others hissed.

Pearl cringed. "Sorry," she said to Jade. "I'm always putting my foot in my big mouth."

Miss Whitestone shook her head at Pearl, but her eyes were soft. They were violet in color, something Topaz had never seen in anyone else, and they crinkled at the corners when she

smiled. "Jade, you're going to join Pearl and Coral's class. Topaz and Opal are in the grade above." Her face fell a little. "Girls, Jade is an orphan, like you. She's been in foster care, but now she's going to live at Breakwater Hall with us."

Topaz and the others exchanged glances. That explained it.

"Come on," said Topaz, taking Jade by the arm. "Look, this one's your bed."

"They're really comfy!" said Pearl.

"And just let me know if my makeup ever takes up too much space," added Coral.

"Not if," said Opal, teasing. "*When!*"

Jade gave a weak smile.

Miss Whitestone beckoned Topaz into the corridor. "I have a favor to ask," she said. "Would you mind including Jade in your boat crew?"

"Of course," Topaz replied. "It'll be a bit of a

squeeze, but we'll manage." Topaz was already thinking of the new arrangements in the boat—where everyone would sit and who would take what role.

"Will you keep a close eye on her too?" asked Miss Whitestone. "My guess is Jade's going to find it difficult to fit in."

Topaz could relate. She was lucky to have such a good group of friends, but they were so different to the other girls at the school—girls who had families and knew where they came from. The only thing Topaz had from her own family was her ring, with its square-shaped, honey-colored stone. She longed to know what it felt like to be loved by a mom and a dad.

"I promise we will," she said. "You know our motto, Miss Whitestone: all friends on deck!"

Topaz walked back into the dorm. Jade looked shell-shocked. Her eyes darted around the room as Opal straightened the sheets on her bed, Coral listed her many nail varnish colors, and Pearl stood at the window, pointing out her favorite picnic spots by the lake.

"So Jade," Topaz called over the noise, "do you sail?"

The others fell silent. The answer to this question was very important.

Jade shook her head. "I've never even been in a boat before."

"Never?" cried Pearl, blond pigtails bouncing as she jumped up and down. "Then you're in for a treat! It's easy, just remember port is left, starboard is right, the bow is the front and the stern is the back."

"Don't worry," said Topaz. "We'll teach you everything you need to know."

Topaz was pleased to see Jade smile—a real smile at last. She'd be part of the crew in no time.

***

Topaz stands in the center of the ballroom, wearing a layered satin sari. The room is decorated with candles, and colorful silk banners are draped from floor to ceiling. The open windows let in the scent of sweet flowers and the calls of tropical birds.

The palace is built into the side of a mountain. Plants grow from the stone walls, waterfalls tumble down into pools, and fountains flow on the ballroom floor. Waiters twirl around the guests, offering them juicy mangoes, grapes, and melons.

A couple stand on a raised platform, both wearing crowns. The dark-haired man—the king, clearly—claps his hands. "Let the dancing begin!" he shouts. Topaz feels a thrill of excitement as a drumbeat starts at the back of the room.

"Topaaaaaz!" someone calls...

***

Topaz woke up. She must have had the same dream a hundred times—it always felt so real, as if it were an actual place rather than a wonderful fantasy.

"Topaaaaaz!"

She sat up in her bed. That wasn't part of the dream! It was a man's voice, deep and booming like thunder. It sounded as if it was coming from the lake. She looked at the clock glowing on her desk: 1.13 a.m. Who could be calling her to the lake now?

She got out of bed and crept to the window. A floorboard creaked. She looked to see if the others had stirred. Opal, Pearl, and Coral were sleeping soundly.

But Jade's bed was empty.

Jade had gone!

Chapter 2

"Girls! Wake up!" Topaz cried, flicking on the lights.

Miss Whitestone had specifically told Topaz to look out for Jade, and she'd disappeared on her very first night!

Pearl groaned as she rolled over.

Coral rubbed her eyes. "Is it morning already?"

"What's the matter?" asked Opal, blinking awake.

"Jade's gone!" Topaz told them. She was

already sliding into her slippers.

Coral, Pearl, and Opal jumped out of their beds and did the same. "We'll find her," said Pearl.

"All friends on deck," said Opal.

They crept out of the room and down the corridor, passing the closed doors of their school friends' dorms. Jade was nowhere to be seen— the only thing out of place was a clean sock that must have fallen from someone's laundry bag. They were halfway down the grand stairway when Topaz heard the voice again. "*Topaaaaaz!*" They all stopped dead.

"You heard it too?" whispered Topaz.

The others nodded. Pearl bit her lip and Coral twirled a lock of hair nervously.

"Why is someone calling me?" asked Topaz.

"Calling you?" asked Opal, her face scrunched up.

"He was calling me," said Pearl.

"No," said Coral. "It was my name."

They looked at each other, frowning in confusion. "We each heard our own names?" said Topaz in surprise.

The others nodded. Topaz took a deep breath.

"This is super creepy," said Coral.

"Maybe he called Jade, too, and that's where she's gone," Opal suggested.

"Good thinking!" said Topaz, starting to make her way down the stairs again. "Let's follow the voice and see where it leads."

Quietly, Topaz lifted the latch on the door leading outside. The night air was thick and humid. Dark clouds loomed overhead. Thunder rumbled somewhere in the distance.

"That doesn't sound good," said Topaz. "Quick, we've got to find her."

They tiptoed past the school's herb garden, then opened the gate to a stairway that zigzagged down to the lakeside. Hedges grew high on either side. Only when they were a few steps from the bottom could they see the lake...and there was a boat on it, rowing out into the deep water! "Is that Jade?" asked Coral.

"It can't be," said Opal. "She said she'd never been in a boat before. Why would she start now, in the middle of the night, all alone?"

"And when there's a massive storm coming?" said Pearl, pointing at the heavy clouds.

Just then, a flash of lightning lit up Jade's face. Topaz ran down the last few steps, calling her name. The others were right behind her, shouting too, but Jade didn't turn. She either couldn't hear or she was ignoring them.

"Head for Nestor!" cried Topaz.

The girls ran to the dock where their boat was moored. As they untied Nestor, thunder crashed and the storm finally broke. Rain tipped down, instantly soaking through Topaz's purple pajamas. Topaz looked at the others, but it was as if the rain didn't exist—they wore determined expressions as they got ready to set sail. Even Coral, who hated what the rain did to her hair, seemed to pay it no notice as they jumped aboard.

"All friends on deck?" asked Topaz.

"Aye aye, Captain!" they chorused back.

"Let's go!" Topaz said.

Like coordinated dancers, the girls pulled the ropes, one hand over the other, so the sails came up quickly. They got up a good speed, but the choppy water and pelting rain made it the hardest sailing Topaz had ever experienced.

Another flash of lightning lit up the sky, and for a second Topaz could see Jade clearly again. Her little rowing boat rocked from side to side, almost capsizing. Jade instinctively put her arms out to steady herself, letting go of the oars.

No! Topaz's heart sank as the oars slid out of the rowlocks and floated away from the boat. Jade twisted this way and that to see where they'd gone.

"Jade! We're nearly there!" Opal called.

Lightning flashed again and at last Jade saw them. Standing up, she waved frantically.

"Sit down!" Topaz shouted. But it was too late.

Jade lurched backward and fell into the lake. Coral, Pearl, and Opal screamed.

Fighting down her own panic, Topaz tried to think like a captain. "Quick! We need to turn into the wind and then drop the sail!"

She could just see Jade's head above the water. Jade was struggling, the waves crashing over her head.

Topaz turned the boat into the howling wind, and Pearl, Coral, and Opal worked as a team to drop the sail.

Jade reached out as they glided closer. "Help!" she spluttered.

Topaz leaned over to grab her. For a millisecond, she was startled by the ring Jade was wearing—a gold band with a green, oval-shaped stone, similar to the ones they all had.

Topaz took Jade's hand and pulled. "I've got you," she said. "Help me!" she called to the others.

With each helping hand, it got easier to bring Jade in. First Pearl grabbed on to her, then Opal,

then Coral—

CRACK!

A blast threw
Topaz backward
across the boat.
There was a flash
of light so bright that
she squeezed her eyes

shut. She wondered if they'd been struck by
lightning, but that couldn't be right—the light
was golden. Then Topaz heard the thuds of her
friends falling beside her.

Several seconds passed before Topaz dared
to open her eyes. When she opened them she
was relieved to see that Jade had made it aboard,
but something was wrong. Instead of their
small boat's familiar plastic bottom, wooden
boards stretched from bow to stern. Three masts
towered over her head, reaching into the dark,

stormy sky. Rain still poured from heavy clouds and thunder rumbled all around, but something about the air had changed. What was it?

"Is everyone OK?" Topaz asked.

Pearl was wide-eyed. Jade looked as green as her eyes. Coral's mouth had fallen open.

"Define OK!" said Opal, her voice shaking.

Topaz suddenly realized what was different about the air—it smelled salty, like seawater.

"I don't think we're on our lake any more."

She took another look at the boat they were on. Flying above the tallest mast was a pink flag with a heart and crossbones on it. This was a pirate ship!

Chapter 3

Topaz looked over the side of the ship but she couldn't see very far. It was the dead of night, storm clouds hid the moon and stars, and wisps of mist scudded across the water.

"Whoa!" said Coral, as she spun around, staring at everything. "Where are we?"

Pearl ran from the port side to the starboard side. "This is too weird," she said, shaking her head.

Opal peered toward the bow. "I don't like the look of these waves."

Jade ran to Topaz and hugged her. She was shaking and soaking wet. "Thank you so much for rescuing me," she said.

"No problem," said Topaz, hugging her back.

Coral and Pearl were beside them now.

"We have this motto," said Pearl, "all friends on deck."

"It means we look out for each other," said Coral, touching Jade on the arm.

Jade pulled a strand of wet hair from her face. "You must think I was stupid to go out on the lake, but I heard this voice calling me."

"We heard it too!" said Coral.

"I think we have something else to worry about," Opal gasped, as a huge wave tipped the boat. The girls grabbed on to each other to stay upright. A sudden boom of thunder shook the air and a crack of lightning illuminated massive waves as far as the eye could see. Jade looked terrified.

Suddenly, Topaz felt the weight of four pairs of eyes on her.

"Why are you looking at me?" she said.

"You're the captain," said Coral.

Topaz bit her lip. Could she captain something this big? She studied the ropes lying on deck and followed them up to the sails. The ropes were thick, almost too thick to get her hand around, but really this boat was just a larger version of their one at school.

The others raced back toward the stern and climbed up to the raised deck that held the ship's wheel. Pearl tried to turn the huge wheel. "It's too heavy!" she shouted.

The friends all pushed together. But the wheel wouldn't budge.

"It's stuck!" shouted Coral.

"Topaz, what do we do?" Opal called.

"*Topaaaaaz!*"

There was that voice again. Topaz whirled around. But she couldn't see anyone, only her four friends.

"Topaz!" the voice said again—deep and booming. "Get to the quarterdeck!"

"Where are you?" she asked. "Who are you?"

The voice sighed impatiently. "The wheel, Topaz."

The voice must be the ship's captain, Topaz decided, as she headed to join the others on the quarterdeck. "Pearl and Opal, tighten the jib sail!"

"The what?" asked Opal, staring around.

"The rope at the bow—starboard side!" the voice commanded. "Coral, climb the rigging to the crow's nest!"

Coral looked up at the height of the mast. "Me?" she said, cringing. "Up there?"

Topaz was on the quarterdeck now and could see the full length of the ship stretching out in front of her. But still no captain.

"Jade!" the voice shouted. "Head to the foredeck."

Jade hesitated.

"At the front!" boomed the voice.

"What are you waiting for, Topaz?" the voice called. "Take the wheel!"

But if the other four girls couldn't move it, working together, how would she do it by herself?

Topaz put her hands on the wooden handles, and readied herself to push with all her might, but the wheel turned easily and the ship instantly changed direction.

"How did you do that?" Opal called over. "That wheel weighs a million tons!"

It felt light as a feather to Topaz. She was just

about to ask Opal if she was joking when Jade shouted from the foredeck. "WAVE!"

The approaching wave was massive, way over the height of the masts. Topaz thought of Coral, up in the crow's-nest. She'd be knocked into the water for sure!

But Coral was standing with her hands on her hips, glaring at the wave. "Oh, will you just STOP!" she shouted.

Immediately, the wave died down, sinking back like a puppy who'd just been told off. The water around them became as calm as Lapis Lake on a summer's day. Even the wind stopped blowing. Topaz almost fell over in surprise. Had the storm suddenly stopped? But no, a few yards away, the waves still thrashed and churned.

"What in the oceans...?" Topaz muttered to herself. Coral couldn't have made that happen, could she?

"We're saved!" shouted Jade.

"How did you do that?" Pearl asked.

"I'm not sure..." said Coral.

Too much weird stuff had happened tonight —the voice calling them, the pirate ship, turning the wheel so easily, Coral stopping the storm... Topaz knew who could give them some answers. "Search the ship," she said. "The captain must be here somewhere."

The others scurried around her, hunting behind barrels and trunks.

"Come to the bow," the voice said.

Topaz climbed up to the foredeck at the front of the ship, but the captain wasn't there.

"Look over the side," said the voice.

Topaz looked, but all she could see was the ship's wooden figurehead, shaped like the head and neck of a black stallion—just like the horse painted on the side of their boat back at school.

"Still can't see you, Captain," she said.

"Then you must need glasses," the figurehead replied, craning around to look at her.

Topaz almost fell overboard with shock. The night was getting weirder and weirder!

"But I'm not the captain," he said. "You're the captain of this ship, Topaz."

Just then, Opal, Jade, Coral, and Pearl appeared by Topaz's side.

"What are you looking at?" Pearl asked her.

Topaz pointed to the grinning figurehead and

Coral shrieked.

"Hey!" the figurehead winced. "I'm made of wood, but I'm not deaf."

"You're Nestor!" said Opal, leaning over to pat him on the neck. "Come to life to take care of us!"

"Oh, stop being soft," Nestor replied. But Topaz saw the way his eyes closed as Opal stroked him. He was enjoying it more than he let on.

"Our boat has turned into a magic pirate ship!" said Pearl, grinning.

"It can't have! Maybe this is a dream," said Opal.

But the deck beneath Topaz's feet felt pretty real.

"I don't know what's going on," said Coral, flipping her hair, a smile emerging on her face. "But it's awesome!"

Topaz shook her head. If she was the captain, she'd have to take charge. She looked around and spotted a telescope fixed to the deck. "We need to find Breakwater Hall, or some landmark which could lead us to safety." said Topaz.

"You can't go," Nestor said. "Lemuria needs you."

"What's Lemuria?" asked Pearl.

"It's a place," Nestor replied.

"A place where?" said Jade.

"Here!" said Nestor.

Topaz put her eye to the telescope and

searched the dark horizon on the starboard side. All she could see was miles of raging water below the night sky.

"How do we get back?" she said, turning the telescope to the port side. Still she could only see miles of ocean, but a dark shape loomed, just visible through the mist. "It's a ship!" she cried. "Maybe they can help us?"

But there was a smaller shape too, flying toward them.

"A parrot!" shrieked Coral.

Topaz wondered what a parrot was doing in the middle of an ocean. And there was something funny about its leg. "Is that...?"

"It's got a wooden leg!" Opal said.

"And an eyepatch," Pearl squealed.

"That's so weird," said Jade, smiling.

"That's so cute!" said Coral.

The parrot squawked. "Jasper's in trouble!

Jasper's in trouble!"

"Who's Jasper?" asked Coral.

"Haven't a clue," said Nestor.

"Maybe it's the name of that ship," said Topaz.
She peered into the telescope again. The ship
was closer now. It was a three-masted ship—like
theirs, only bigger. The mists parted, and through
the darkness she saw a
plank sticking out from
the side of the ship.

"There's a
boy on a plank,"
Topaz told the
others. He
looked about
their age.
"He must be
Jasper." A
woman stepped

up behind him. She was tall and bony, her black cape billowing around her in the storm. She held a long, golden staff with a glinting black stone at the end. The boy raised his chin defiantly as the woman used the staff to poke him forward.

"She's making him walk the plank!" cried Coral.

Topaz clenched her fists. "We have to save him!" she cried. "All friends on deck!"

Chapter 4

Jasper stood quivering on the edge of the plank. Beyond the circle of calm that surrounded Nestor, the sea still raged. If the woman pushed him in he'd drown for sure.

"We have to go back into the storm," Topaz said to the others. The parrot landed on Topaz's shoulder, squawking in approval.

But Jade's green eyes were wide with fear. "Are you crazy?"

"We have to get closer to save Jasper. And the only way to get to him quickly is by using the wind," Topaz explained. "There's none here."

"I know!" said Jade, cringing. "That's why I like it!"

Topaz smiled at her. "Together we can handle this," she said. "You stay here and keep a lookout."

Jade steeled herself and put her eye to the telescope.

Topaz was already running back to the wheel as she shouted out instructions, "Pearl, take the sails on the foremast. Opal, the sails on the main mast. Coral, you've got the mast at the back."

"The mizzen mast," Nestor informed her.

Back at the helm, Topaz steered the ship into the storm again, wincing as the rain lashed against her skin. Her belly turned as the ship rose then fell sharply over the waves. But the parrot stayed on her shoulder, which comforted her a little.

"Jasper's in trouble," it squawked over

and over.

"Don't worry, little buddy," she whispered in reply. "We'll save him!"

They had soon closed in on the other ship enough for Topaz to get a clearer view of the woman through the mist—she had dark purple hair and wore a golden crown. Her scowl was deep and terrifying, and made Topaz wonder if she'd ever smiled in her life. As well as her golden staff, the woman held a big piece of paper.

"Hey, Nestor!" Topaz called. "Is that the queen of this Lemuria place?"

Nestor scoffed. "She wishes!"

Behind the woman stood two men. One was tall and skinny, with a thin black mustache. The other was wider than he was tall, and wearing a waistcoat bursting at the buttons. Jasper had brown messy hair and a backpack on his back. He caught sight of Nestor and grinned, as if he

had always known someone would save him.

"Stay away!" the woman shouted. "I am Obsidian!"

"Never heard of you!" Coral shouted back from her place at the mizzen mast, hands on hips. "Go," Obsidian yelled, sounding even angrier, "or I'll wreck that puny ship of yours!"

"Not again," Nestor muttered.

"We're not going to let you make that boy walk the plank!" Opal shouted.

"We're not afraid of you!" Pearl added.

"Speak for yourself, Pearl," Topaz whispered, her heart pounding. But she joined in. "Let the boy go!"

Obsidian's face cracked into a cruel smile. "But that was my plan all along," she said with a chuckle. Then with an almighty shove, she pushed Jasper along the plank.

Topaz gasped, but at the end of the plank

Topaz
The Sunken Treasure

Jasper jumped. He somersaulted in the air while Obsidian's mouth fell open in surprise. The skinny henchman tried to catch him, but his arms closed around thin air as Jasper grabbed a dangling rope, snatched the piece of paper from Obsidian's hands, then swung through the air toward Nestor.

"He's not going to make it!" said Coral.

"Oh yes he will!" said Topaz. She raced to the edge of the ship, and as he flew toward her, she stretched out and grabbed his arm. Jasper smashed against the side of the ship, but Topaz wasn't going to let him fall. She pulled him on board as if he weighed nothing.

"Hi," he said, a cheeky grin on his face.

"You must be Jasper," Topaz said, grinning back.

The parrot left her shoulder and landed on the boy's. "I see you've met Pegleg," Jasper said.

Behind them Obsidian let out an almighty screech. "Fire the cannons!"

"Uh oh," said Pearl.

"Incoming!" Jade cried from the front of the ship.

Topaz turned to see a cannonball hurtling toward them. "Hit the decks!" she shouted.

Topaz and Jasper dropped to the deck and the cannonball flew over their heads.

"Darn cannons," Jasper cursed.

"They aren't the only ones with a pirate ship," Opal called over. "Nestor, what's the cannon situation?"

"We do have cannons..." Nestor said. "But... they're a bit...erm...rusty. Haven't worked for years."

There was a sudden cry behind Topaz and she turned to see Jade sprinting below deck. But there was no time to go after her.

A minute later, a deafening BOOM shook the ship. A cannonball shot out of the gun deck below at top speed. It flew straight for Obsidian's ship—and tore through its main sail!

"Yesssss!" Topaz gave a fist pump. Jade must have got a cannon working!

The other girls were open-mouthed. "How did Jade do that, if the cannons were all rusted up?" asked Opal.

"Beats me," said Coral, "but I'm glad she did."

Another boom, this time from Obsidian's ship, stopped their celebration. Seconds later, a cannonball smashed into their hull. Topaz was thrown off her feet. Planks and splinters of wood flew through the air. It was a direct hit!

"Owww!" shouted Nestor. "That stings!"

"Jade!" cried Topaz, and she jumped up and ran below deck to see if she was OK.

Only dim moonlight shone in through the

small openings in the ship's sides where two rows of eight cannons pointed out. It took a moment for Topaz's eyes to adjust. She was relieved to see Jade getting up from the floor, rubbing her ears.

"Are you all right?"

Jade winced. "I'm OK," she said, dusting splinters of wood from her pajamas.

The gun deck was above sea level, but the rough seas gushed water in through the hole Obsidian's cannonball had made.

"I'll rig something up to get the water out," Jade told her. "You just get us away from Obsidian, OK?"

"How bad is it?" Opal asked as Topaz raced toward the wheel.

"Pretty bad! But they've got a hole in their main sail—we should be faster." Topaz replied.

Topaz turned the ship's wheel, "Let's go!" she

cried at the top of her voice.

The wind caught the sails instantly, billowing

them out. The ship raced through the sea at a speed Topaz had never sailed before. Her hair was blown back, and she couldn't help smiling as Obsidian's ship disappeared from view. As the sun cracked through the horizon, shedding pink light all around, Topaz realized she'd never felt as alive as she did right now—on this pirate ship, cutting through the rough waves like a cutlass through

silk, her best friends around her.

She looked out to the sea and smiled.

This is where I belong.

Chapter 5

The sea was calm at last. Light glinted on the tips of the waves and Obsidian's ship was far behind. Topaz and her friends were safe...as long as they could get to land before they took on too much water. Topaz knew that Jade, still below deck, would call if they were in real trouble. But right now there were other things on her mind.

"Hey, girls," Topaz called. "Ease the sails and come here."

One by one Pearl, Coral, and Opal met Topaz, Jasper, and Pegleg on the quarterdeck.

"We need answers," Topaz said to Jasper.

"Yeah," said Pearl, pulling her pigtails tighter. "What in the oceans is going on?"

"Where to start?" said Jasper, as he pulled a nut from his pocket and threw it to Pegleg on his shoulder. The parrot caught it and started eating.

"How about telling us why Obsidian was firing cannons at us?" said Opal. "And why was she trying to kill you?"

"Obsidian wants to rule Lemuria," said Jasper. "But she can't without this."

Jasper pulled the piece of paper he'd snatched from Obsidian out of his backpack. It was a map—five large islands were dotted around the edges, with one smaller island in the center. "This is a very important, very magical map. It marks where the old kings and queens hid the Treasures that protected Lemuria."

They all leaned closer to look. Topaz took in

the names of the islands—*The White Isle, The Orange Isle, The Green Isle, The Purple Isle,* and *The Pink Isle.* The central island was very small— no more than the size of a coin on the map—*The Island of the Five Thrones.* Topaz touched the thick, rough paper and the place beneath her finger suddenly grew larger, while the rest of the map shrunk.

"Whoa!" said Coral. "I've never seen a map do that before."

"I told you it was magical." Jasper grinned proudly. "My parents made it." His face fell. "Which is why Obsidian captured them."

"That's awful," said Coral, her hand flying to her mouth.

"She captured all of us," Jasper continued. "But I managed to escape with the map."

"I don't understand," said Topaz. "How would these...Treasures...or whatever, help her rule?"

Jasper's eyebrows bunched together. "Because they're the magical *Treasures of Lemuria*...everyone knows that!"

Topaz subtly shook her head at the girls— now was not the time to tell him how much they didn't know.

"We've been...away," she said.

Jasper raised one eyebrow, but carried on anyway. "Obsidian rules already, but with fear. If she had the Treasures she'd be able to control the spirit of each island, and make everyone do whatever she wanted."

Topaz thought of the scowl on Obsidian's face. She wouldn't want that woman to be her teacher, let alone in charge of a whole island!

"It never used to be like this." Jasper touched the central island—*The Island of the Five Thrones*—and it grew larger on the map. Topaz saw that it was a single mountain—a volcano, perhaps. "This is where the five families would come together to govern Lemuria peacefully…" Jasper trailed off. "Before Obsidian killed them."

Topaz could tell that whoever these royal families were, Jasper wished they were still alive.

"The Treasures need to be set in the five crowns of the rulers in order to keep the islands safe. Before they died, the royal families hid the Treasures, so Obsidian would never find them. The islands of Lemuria are suffering, but things would be a lot worse if Obsidian had the Treasures in her clutches."

"You keep talking about Lemuria," said Opal, pointing to the map. "But what ocean is this?"

Jasper raised his eyebrows again. "This is the only ocean. This is a map of the whole world."

The girls looked at each other.

Pearl scratched her head. "But where is—"

"Ahem." Nestor interrupted.

"But how can—" started Coral

"Ahem," Nestor tried again.

"This can't be—" Opal said.

"AHEM!" Nestor shouted. "Does anyone care that I'm sinking?"

Topaz's eyes went wide. The gun deck! Jade! "Jasper, do you know anyone who can fix our ship?"

Jasper nodded. "There's someone on the Orange Isle who might help."

"If we can get there before we sink," Nestor added.

Topaz and the others raced down to the gun deck to help Jade. Water gushed through the hole made by the cannonball. Jade was up to her ankles, attaching some piping together and fixing it to more pipes that ran along the floor and out of the hole.

"Are you OK?" asked Pearl.

Jade nodded, but didn't stop work.

"What's this?"Opal asked, pointing at the pipes.

"It's getting the water out," Jade explained. "I made a pump out of some stuff I found lying around and—"

"You made a pump?!" Topaz exclaimed. "How?"

Jade looked up for the first time. "It's weird, it's like a blueprint just appeared in front of my eyes, and suddenly I knew how to make it. Same thing with the cannons."

That didn't seem possible to Topaz, but she watched as Jade turned a handle and water squirted out of the ship and into the ocean.

"Wow," said Topaz. *Jade must be super-smart!*
The girls took turns on the handle. The deck
started to clear of water, and eventually Topaz felt
sure they weren't going to sink.

"Land ahoy!" called Nestor. "Finally."

The girls gathered around an open gun port.
Sure enough, in the near distance, an island
loomed into view.

"This won't do at all," said Coral.

"What's the matter?" Jade asked her.

"We're still in our pajamas!"

Topaz had totally forgotten! She was still in
the pajamas that she'd woken up in and so were
the rest of the girls! Opal wore her zebra-print
pyjamas, Coral's had hearts, Pearl's had shells,
and Jade's were the same shade of green as
her eyes.

"Check the captain's cabin," Nestor called.

They ran upstairs, raced into the cabin and shut the door. There was a table with nautical maps, and a few leather bottles. In one corner was a trunk. Coral threw it open and squealed with delight. "Whoa, there's so much amazing stuff in here!" She started throwing out clothes. "Jade, try this. Opal, this is perfect for you. Oh, there's a nice dress here for you, Pearl. Actually no, this one's better."

Topaz looked at her options. She was tempted by a sari made of silks so delicate that they swirled, even in the light breeze. It was similar to the one from her dream. But the silk would rip too easily. No, she needed something more practical. She put on a purple shirt that was a bit baggy and found a blue top. Then, she picked out a pair of pants and some boots—they fitted perfectly! Finally, she wrapped a ribbon around her head to keep her hair out of her eyes.

Coral examined her. "Just one finishing touch." She stepped forward and put a gold hoop earring in Topaz's ear.

Topaz felt ready for anything. She turned to look in the mirror.

"I look like a pirate," she said, grinning.

Topaz turned to her friends. Opal wore a dress and a waistcoat, and a belt with a golden buckle looping her waist. Coral tied a handkerchief around Opal's thick black hair. Pearl had three-quarter length pants and a short-sleeved shirt. Jade put on a green jacket and boots—clearly her favorite color. Coral tied a green ribbon to the hat Jade wore. "Thanks Coral," said Jade.

Coral looked great too. A pink jacket over a long, layered skirt—a ribbon around her neck and a matching one in her hair. Her outfit brought out the freckles on her skin. "Almost..." she muttered as she examined herself in the mirror. She found a hefty pair of scissors in a drawer, and cut into her skirt so it sat just above her knees. "*Now* we're ready for the island."

They burst out of the captain's cabin. "What do you think, Jasper?" Topaz asked.

Coral did a twirl and threw one hand into the air. "Ta-dah!"

Jasper's jaw dropped.

"My fashion skills have never had this effect before!" Coral said with a grin.

But Jasper wasn't looking at their clothes, he was looking at their hands. "Show me your rings," he said.

Each of them held up their right hand.

Jasper put his hand to his mouth. "You're the princesses!"

"What are you talking about?" Topaz asked.

"I told you about the five royal families," he said. The girls nodded. "Before Obsidian attacked

them, they made a plan with the seawitch,
Celestine. She protected their daughters by
sending them away."

This sounded like a fairy tale to Topaz.

"Celestine left Lemuria to find the princesses

...but not before promising that one day the princesses would return, find the Treasures, and save the kingdoms."

"What's that got to do with us?" said Opal.

"You're the princesses," said Jasper, his face

bursting into a smile. "You have the rings of the royal families!"

Topaz shook her head. *Princesses? What rubbish!*

Pearl jumped up and down. "I'm a princess!" she cried.

Coral twirled her hair thoughtfully. "I always knew it," she said.

Opal shook her head. "This is just silly."

Jade just bit her nails. She looked like Coral did when she was tackling algebra homework.

"Oh," Jasper said. "I should probably..." He bowed low.

Topaz pulled him upright. "Don't be ridiculous," she said. "We've seen a lot today, sure. New worlds, talking pirate ships, one-legged parrots..." Pegleg gave a squawk. "But princesses? No way!"

"Think about it, Topaz," said Coral. "We've

always had these rings, but we've never known where they came from."

"And we seem to have weird powers now," said Jade. "I can fix things."

"Coral stopped the storm," said Pearl.

Topaz thought about the way she'd turned the wheel when the others couldn't, and how easily she'd pulled Jasper on board. Could they really be magical princesses?

"I'm not sure," Topaz said.

"Well I'm sure," Jasper said. "And Lemuria needs you!" He pointed to where the Orange Isle lay, just a few hundred yards away. "Let me show you why."

Chapter 6

Nestor sailed slowly into the stone harbor. Topaz was mesmerized. Boats of all sizes were unloading wooden crates and barrels, from small rowing boats and fishing boats to ships almost as large as Nestor. But looking closer, Topaz could see that the boats were battered, their sails frayed. The fishermen were quiet and unhappy. The crews unloading their merchandise looked thin and weary. The Orange Isle was suffering, just as Jasper had said.

"Orange Isle, Orange Isle," squawked Pegleg

as Jasper tossed him a nut.

A mountain range loomed over the harbor, the peaks glowing orange in the sunshine. Beyond the harbor was a busy boardwalk with stores and stalls, and the merchants looked just as haggard as the people on the ships.

"I've never seen anything like it!" called Pearl.

"Me neither," said Coral. "Not even in movies."

Above the stores, a building of columns and windows and ornate balconies had been carved into the mountain.

"What's that?" Topaz asked Jasper.

"You'll see..." he replied. There was a look in his eye that Topaz didn't quite understand.

They found a space to moor and Topaz used a rope to secure the ship.

Jade was just behind her. "Dry land!" she said. "I could kiss it."

Topaz smiled at her, and began tying the

rest of the ship's ropes to the mooring posts. A gangplank lowered next to her.

"There you go, princesses," said Nestor.

Coral, Pearl, Opal, and Jasper walked down, wide-eyed.

"This is so cool," said Coral.

"Look at all the cute animals everywhere," said Opal. There were lots of cats around the harbor, sniffing in buckets, looking for food. There were a few stray dogs too—and orange crabs clung to the rocks below.

A black-and-white cat trotted over and rubbed Opal's legs in a figure of eight. Then Opal and the cat appeared to start talking to each other!

Topaz laughed, but the cat meowed, looking directly at Opal.

"I'm afraid not," Opal said, frowning as if replying to a serious request. "We weren't on a

Topaz

The Sunken Treasure

fishing trip so we don't have any."

Topaz stood frozen. "Wait...did that cat...speak to you?" she asked Opal.

Opal tilted her head to the side. "Yeah, I guess animals speak here." Her eyes went wide. "Didn't you understand it?"

The girls all shook their heads.

"Oh." Opal seemed as surprised as the rest of them. "It spoke just as clearly as you do."

Topaz couldn't believe it.

"Hey!" said Pearl. "Now you *all* have magic powers! Coral controls the elements. Jade's super-brainy. Topaz's super-strong. Opal's chatting with cats. What's my special power?"

Jade cringed. She looked at the others, who all shrugged. "Sorry, Pearl."

Pearl sighed and her shoulders slumped. "Not fair," she sulked.

Coral turned to Jasper. "So...where's this boat

fixer person you said you knew?"

"Follow me." he said.

Jasper led the way through the town. A pretty three-tiered fountain stood in the central square, engraved with leaves and people carrying fruit. It looked like the one in Topaz's recurring dream—only this fountain was dry and empty.

Jasper jumped up onto a crumbling stone bench. "Barney! Barney!" he cried, searching the crowds. "It's the princesses! The saviors of Lemuria!"

Topaz snapped out of her trance. Everyone turned to look at them, and she felt her cheeks burning.

"Jasper!" she hissed.

"Should we really be telling everyone this?" asked Opal.

People began to come closer. A woman carrying a basket of clean clothes walked toward them, her skirt in rags, her free arm outstretched. "Can it be true?" she said.

Coral curtsied. "Princess Coral, at your service," she said.

The woman beamed. "It is them!" she cried.

People dropped what they were doing to run over. Some bowed low. Another woman clapped her hands together in glee, and the three young children at her feet did the same. The crowd grew larger, but some people were frowning.

"They're not the princesses," a gruff man growled.

"They are!" said a younger woman carrying a pot on her head. "I can feel it!"

Pearl stepped in front of Coral and bowed low, flourishing one arm in the air. "I'm Princess Pearl!" she announced.

Topaz pulled Pearl up straight, and yanked Coral toward her. "We don't know if we're the princesses," she whispered. "We do know that we need someone to fix our ship!"

A white-bearded man wearing a navy hat pushed through the crowd. His skin was sun-beaten as if he'd spent every day of his long life outside, and he had a pipe in his mouth.

"Barney!" shouted Jasper, and he jumped off the bench and wrapped his arms around the man. "I've found the princesses!"

Barney pulled the pipe from his mouth and assessed Topaz, Opal, Jade, Coral, and Pearl. "Well, blow me down," he said. Tears welled up in his eyes. "I've been waiting for you ever since the dark day when Obsidian took over. This island has been getting worse and worse. It never rains. Nothing grows. We don't have much food. But the seawitch said you'd return, and here you are..."

Topaz felt sorry for them all—their desperate faces, their thin bodies—but what could they do to fix it? She stepped forward and shook his hand. "Hello, Barney. Jasper said you might be able to help us. We took a cannonball to our ship fighting Obsidian."

There was a collective gasp from the crowd.

"Careful," a woman in the crowd hissed. "Obsidian's spies are everywhere."

"It would be an honor to fix your boat," said Barney.

We're probably not the princesses, Topaz thought, *but there are some perks to people thinking you're royalty!*

After Jasper showed Barney the hole in Nestor, Topaz wanted to look around the island; but before they had gone far they heard screaming. The five girls looked down a side alley to see two men with giant dogs on leads. They were throwing over stalls and smashing everything in sight. The stallholders cowered and cried in terror as the dogs growled and snapped at them.

One of the men was tall and skinny with a thin mustache, the other wide with a waistcoat. Topaz recognized the men from Obsidian's ship! Obsidian must have landed on the other side of the island.

"They should hold those dogs back!" Topaz shouted angrily, hands on her hips.

"They aren't dogs," said Opal. "They're wolves!"

Jade shook her head. "They're not getting away with this."

"Too right!" said Topaz, starting to walk toward the men.

"Stop!" said Jasper, as he grabbed Topaz by the elbow. "That's Larry and Boil—Obsidian's men. You're the princesses. You need to be kept safe!"

"If I *am* a princess," Topaz told him, "I'm not *that* kind of princess." She stomped off toward the men and was pleased to see her friends right there with her.

"Stop that now!" shouted Topaz, sounding braver than she really felt.

"Yeah!" said Pearl. "Bullies!"

The tall one—Larry—looked up at them, shocked for a moment. Then he smiled, his thin mustache pointing upward. "Why, if it isn't a troupe of little girls!"

"How dare you speak that way to the Princesses of Lemuria?" said Jasper.

"Princesses?" Larry's mouth fell open.

Jasper gulped.

Larry narrowed his eyes. "Snarl! Menace!" he said to the wolves. "Get them!"

Topaz exchanged a grimace with the other girls. Now wasn't the time to stand and fight,

now was the time to…"Run!" she yelled. No one needed telling twice. Jasper and the girls ran with her, Pegleg flying overhead, but the wolves weren't far behind.

"Opal!" Jade shouted. "Tell those wolves to stop chasing us!"

"Good idea!" said Opal. "Why are you chasing us?" she called over her shoulder. "Stop!"

All Topaz could hear was the wolves snarling and snapping behind them, but Opal seemed to understand.

"They just keep saying they have to obey their masters. I think they're under a spell," said Opal breathing hard.

"What can we do?" asked Jasper.

"Run faster!" shouted Topaz.

Topaz turned down an alleyway that led them to the foothills of the mountains. They began to clamber up a dry and dusty slope. Topaz caught a glimpse of an entrance to a cave behind a clump of dead trees. "In here quick!" she called.

Running into the dark cave, they pressed themselves against the walls, just as Larry and Boil rushed past.

"We've lost the princesses!" said Larry.

"It's your fault," said Boil. "You can explain it to Obsidian."

Topaz's heart sank. The last thing they needed was Obsidian thinking they were the princesses—she was already angry enough!

Once the sounds of the men and their wolves had died away, Pearl asked, "Everyone OK?"

"Define OK," Opal replied, panting.

"What should we do now?" Jade whispered. "If we go back out of the cave, they'll see us."

Topaz tried to think. A tiny ray of light was coming from the other end of the cave.

"Look," she said. "Maybe there's another

way out?"

Topaz, Jasper, and the girls hurried deeper into the cave. Even though the rest of the island was so dry, the ground here was muddy and wet. When the mud under their feet became smooth stone Topaz realized they were walking through a gully.

"It's as if a river once ran through here," said Jade.

"And disappeared into this cave," added Opal.

"Well, that explains the mud!" moaned Coral, looking in horror at the splodges of brown on her outfit.

Soon, the tiny ray of light became a large beam, and at last they stepped through a stone archway and into a room. It was a grand hall, stretching the length of a tennis court. Columns held up the ceiling, and the ornate windows were broken so the warm air rushed in. Looking around, Topaz saw that parts of the walls had collapsed into rubble, and a film of dust covered everything. The once beautiful room was long-deserted.

"It's a palace!" said Pearl.

"Carved into the mountain!" added Coral.

Topaz saw another fountain, its sides carved with flowers and figures carrying trays of fruit and jugs of wine. This was the palace from her dream! She looked for the waterfalls, but there was nothing but a trickle of water dribbling slowly down the gully—no plants grew from the walls, no sweet flowers filled the air with scent.

A portrait of a woman and a bearded man, both wearing crowns, stared down from one of the remaining walls. They had the same auburn hair as Topaz.

"Who are they?" Pearl wondered aloud.

But Topaz knew. Something deep in her heart told her. These were her parents. There was a lump in her throat and she tried to swallow it down.

"Is this my island?" Topaz asked Jasper, even though she already knew the answer.

Jasper nodded. "Welcome home, Princess Topaz."

Chapter 7

Topaz walked slowly toward the two thrones at the end of the grand hall.

"Are you OK, Topaz?" Opal asked.

Her friends' faces were full of concern.

Topaz nodded. "It's just so weird to think that my parents once sat on these thrones," she said.

"Now they're yours," Jasper said.

But Topaz couldn't think about that.

Topaz sat carefully on one of the crumbling stone thrones. The wooden armrests were carved to look like vines, but they were damp and rotten.

Topaz touched them and a section fell away.

"It must have been beautiful once," she breathed.

"It was," said Jasper. "Just like the rest of the island."

"What happened?" asked Pearl.

"Obsidian attacked this island—all the islands," Jasper explained, "so the royal families hid the magical Treasures. But while the Treasures aren't in the royal crowns, the islands are slowly losing their spirits. Gradually, over the years, the water has dried up here on the Orange

Isle; the plants and animals are dying. Who knows how long the people can survive?"

Topaz sat up straight. If she was the princess, then these were her people. "It's up to me to save them," she said.

"And us!" said Opal, and the rest of the girls nodded. Even Pegleg squawked his support.

Topaz smiled. "What do we need to do?"

"We need to get the Treasure back into the crown," said Jasper. "As we have the map"—he pulled it out of his backpack—"it'll be easy."

Topaz took the map from Jasper to get a closer look. As soon as she held it, the orange stone on her ring lit up. Topaz dropped the map in shock, and the ring went dull again.

"Whoa!" said Coral.

Topaz picked up the map, and again her ring lit up. Suddenly a glowing X magically appeared.

"That must be where the Treasure is hidden!" said Jade.

"It's right here on the island!" said Opal.

"X marks the spot!" said Pearl, jumping up and down.

Topaz stood up and grinned. "So what are we waiting for?"

"Here," said Opal, "I'm good at reading maps." She held out her hand.

Topaz handed it over. "Where to?" she asked.

Opal started walking, her face buried in the map. "This way..."

They walked out of the throne room and down a long, wide corridor. Statues and portraits lined the walls. They turned a corner, into a smaller corridor with lots of doors coming off it. Topaz saw drawing rooms and bedchambers with their furniture and contents turned over or thrown around. Topaz felt her anger rise.

"I bet Larry and Boil did this!" she said.

Jasper nodded. "They're constantly searching for the Treasures. They won't give up until they find them."

"Well bad luck," said Coral. "We have the map and they don't."

Opal pushed a door that led into a much smaller room. "The map says we go in here," she said.

Topaz felt the temperature drop. The room she stepped into was about as big as one of the classrooms at school. Swords and suits of armor hung on the stone walls. There was even a boat with an oar hung up...but no sign of where to go next.

"Dead end," squawked Pegleg.

Topaz clenched her fists in frustration.

Jade looked at the boat on the wall. "Why keep a boat inside a mountain?"

Opal frowned down at the map. "It's as if we're supposed to be on a river."

Topaz saw a blue line snaking across the paper. She listened for the sound of water, but there was nothing. "Could the map be wrong?"

"Not a chance," said Jasper through gritted teeth.

Topaz knew Jasper was protective of the map because his parents made it. But where were they supposed to go?

Just then she heard a deep, rumbling sound coming from the middle of the mountain.

"What was that?" asked Coral.

Immediately, a crack began to spread across the stone floor.

"Earthquake!" shouted Opal.

The crack in the middle of the room got bigger and bigger: Pearl, Jade, and Topaz on one side, Coral, Opal, and Jasper on the other. Pegleg flew above them.

As the crack got wider, Topaz could see that it was filled with rushing water.

"It's a river!" she gasped. "We need that boat!" Jade and Pearl frantically tried to pull it from the wall. Topaz joined them.

"Come on Topaz, use your super-strength!" said Jade.

But no matter how hard Topaz pulled, the boat wouldn't budge. "It's not coming off!" she said, frustrated. Maybe she wasn't super-strong after all?

"The crack's widening!" shouted Coral, from the other side of the room.

"Soon we'll be in the water!" cried Jade.

Topaz gave up pulling. "There must be another way," she said. And then she saw it—a tiny square hole in the wall, just beside the boat. She knew that shape so well. "I've got it!"

"Whatever you've got," said Jade, "can you do it, like, right now please?!"

Topaz pushed her ring into the hole and...a perfect fit! Something clicked. The boat fell from the wall and Topaz caught it.

"Yes!" her friends cried.

Topaz carried the boat above her head and placed it in the water. She held tight while her friends leaped in—first Opal, then Jasper, followed by Coral, Pearl, and Jade. Just as the last bit of floor fell away, Topaz leaped in after them, carrying the oar.

Instantly, the rushing rapids took them down through the crack that had formed in the far wall. Beyond, the water flowed into an underground river. They were traveling at speed, deep into the center of the mountain. Cold wind stung Topaz's face and the freezing spray gave her goosebumps. The rapids swept them this way and that. Topaz

tightened her jaw and went
into captain mode.

"Lean against the
waves!" she cried.

She used the single
oar like a rudder,
steering to the
center of the
river, away
from the rocks.

"Left!" she
cried. Her crew
leaned left and they whooshed around a bend.
They were going as fast as any rollercoaster she'd
ever been on. "Left again," she called.

The boat tilted wildly, but by leaning together
they managed to avoid capsizing.

Finally, the river widened and the boat
slowed a little.

"What is this place?" said Pearl.

The cavern they floated through was vast. Cracks in the ceiling high above let in shafts of light. There was something beautiful and eerie about it—marble lines in the stone made everything sparkle.

"We must be under the mountain range we saw when we arrived," said Jade. "I didn't know mountains had rivers inside them."

"This one does," said Jasper. "The people of the Orange Isle always loved plants and flowers ...before everything started dying. The mountain is very special. It's supposed to watch over and protect them."

"That's why they chose the mountain to protect the Treasure, I bet," said Pearl.

"And the Treasure is really close," said Opal. "Look, the X on the map is just ahead."

Topaz felt safe and protected here too...until

she heard a thundering sound.

"What's that?" said Jade, her green eyes full of panic.

"Sounds like an audience clapping," said Coral.

"Sounds like cars on a freeway," said Opal.

Topaz shook her head. "Sounds like water... falling water!"

Ahead, the river disappeared in a cloud of mist and spray. From the sound of it, this was a very, very large waterfall.

Pegleg squawked above them. "*Abandon ship! Abandon ship!*"

Chapter 8

"It's too late!" shouted Topaz. "We're going over!"

As the boat surged toward the edge of the waterfall, Topaz grabbed the nearest hands to her—Pearl's and Jasper's. Now Topaz could see a pool far, far below—the waterfall was as high as Breakwater Hall!

"Jump!" cried Topaz as the boat tipped over the falls. The six friends leaped from the raft as it spun upside down in the air.

"Whoooooooooa!" they all screamed.

Topaz
The Sunken Treasure

Topaz felt as if she was falling for ages. She lost grip of the hands she was holding and hit the water hard. The shocking coldness took away her breath, as she plunged deeper and deeper. *Where were her friends? Would they all make it?*

Kicking until her legs burned with effort, Topaz swam for the surface. Finally, she broke through and sucked in a lungful of air.

Topaz looked around, straining to see if her friends were all right. The huge waterfall made the pool choppy and she had to kick hard just to stay afloat. Then she saw Pearl's blond head surface and swam toward her.

"Are you OK?" Topaz shouted over the noise of the waterfall.

Pearl coughed up water. "Fine," she gasped.

"Where are the others?" said Topaz as she looked around frantically. She remembered how uncertain Jade was every time they got near the water. Could Jade even swim?

"I'll see if I can find them!" Pearl spluttered above the waves.

"No," said Topaz. "Let's get to the shore. It'll be easier to spot them."

Topaz swam as fast and hard as she could, and hauled herself on to the rocky shore. Panting, she looked for her missing friends. There was no way out except back the way they came.

Her heart raced as she spotted Coral, Opal, Jasper, and then Jade dotted around the rocks and reeds that surrounded the pool. Coral sat with her legs in the water, pushing her hair from her face. Opal was with Jade, her arm around her.

"Is everyone all right?" Topaz called out.

Coral gave a thumbs up. Jade and Opal nodded. Jasper managed to raise his head, but Pearl was still out in the water. She was looking intently at something below the surface.

The moment of relief quickly passed and Topaz let out a frustrated cry. "Arrrrrrgh! We followed the map, but where did it get us?" she cried.

"It got us soaked, that's where!" said Opal, holding the wet map and scowling at it.

Somewhere in the distance, Topaz heard the howl of a wolf. Larry and Boil! Once they got the news to Obsidian that the princesses were here with the map, she'd be after them.

But Topaz was too angry with herself to be afraid. She walked back to the waterfall and started climbing the rocks.

"Where are you going?" Coral called out to her.

"I'm going to see where we went wrong," Topaz said. She put her foot on a stone and stepped up. "Maybe I missed where we were supposed to branch off the river," she said, pulling herself higher with her hands.

"The map doesn't show any forks," Opal said, clambering over to Topaz.

But Topaz didn't stop. "Then the map is stupid," she growled.

"Don't blame the map!" said Jasper, sounding hurt. He was climbing right behind her.

"If it's not the map," said Topaz, "it's me!" She was almost at the top now, finding finger and toeholds between the rocks to help her climb.

"Don't say that!" said Jade, climbing too.

"I'm no *savior princess*." said Topaz. "And I'm certainly not a pirate captain if this is the mess I get my crew into!"

"Don't blame yourself," said Coral, wet hair pulled back.

"How can I not? It's just like the race on Lapis Lake. I'm supposed to be the captain and I've led you all to a dead end."

"We must be on the right path," said Opal, climbing quickly. "We're just...missing something..."

Topaz sighed as she got to the top of the waterfall. "X marks the spot," she said, over and over again. She stretched out a hand to help up first Opal, then Jasper, then Jade, then Coral. "Wait, where's Pearl?" gasped Topaz.

Topaz looked over the edge. Pearl was still in the pool. "Pearl! What are you...hey!"

The pool they'd been swept into—the pool where Pearl was swimming as if she didn't have a care in the world—was in the shape of a massive X!

"Look!" cried Topaz.

Coral clapped her hands in delight.

"I can't believe we didn't see it before!" said Opal.

"I told you the map was right," said Jasper.

"It's so clever! X marks the spot!" Topaz said, grabbing Jasper in a tight squeeze. "I'll never doubt the map again!"

Topaz released him and looked down once more. There was something twinkling in the pool. A thrill ran up Topaz's spine. "Guys, can you see... it must be the Treasure!"

"Pearl!" Coral was calling. "Come up and see this!"

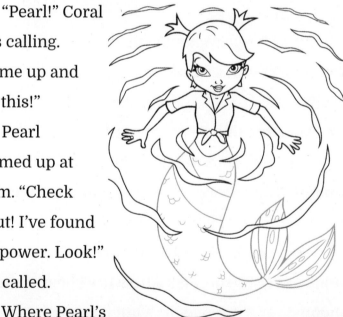

Pearl beamed up at them. "Check it out! I've found my power. Look!" she called.

Where Pearl's legs had been was a shining, purple-green fishtail.

"I'm a mermaid!" she cried. "How cool is that!" Jasper was wide-eyed. Topaz clapped. "Princess Pearl the mermaid!"

Only Jade was quiet, fiddling with something in her hands. Maybe she was nervous.

A wolf howl rang out, this time closer. The friends stopped smiling. Larry and Boil were closing in.

"Pearl!" Topaz shouted urgently. "Can you dive to see what's twinkling at the bottom of the pool?"

"Will do," said Pearl, saluting.

They all stood silently, waiting for Pearl to emerge. Topaz hoped that, with her tail, Pearl could swim strongly enough to fight the currents.

Pearl was back within a minute, no sign of being out of breath. "It's a treasure chest," Pearl shouted up. "I tried to lift it but it's too heavy."

The girls all turned expectantly to Topaz.

But Topaz swallowed uncertainly. Yes, she'd turned the ship's wheel, pulled Jasper aboard, and carried a boat. But swimming with a wooden chest underwater was a completely different prospect.

She clenched her fists. "I've got to try," she said. "It's my family's Treasure. It's my island. I have to save it."

As she stepped forward, Opal grabbed her arm. "You know, Topaz," she said. "Just because you're the captain, it doesn't mean you have to do everything by yourself."

"Yeah," said Coral. "We've got you."

Jade looked up from whatever she was fiddling with. "What was that thing you guys taught me? 'All friends on deck', remember?"

A wave of warmth spread over Topaz. She had her friends by her side, and they'd help her do anything. Topaz pulled the girls in for a tight hug.

"I want to help too!" said Jasper.

The wolves howled again.

"Good," said Topaz. "Because there's no time to lose!"

Chapter 9

Coral went to the edge of the waterfall. She held out both arms and closed her eyes. "Caaaaaaalm," she said. Then she opened one eye. "Please."

The waterfall slowed, as if a tap had been turned. The water in the pool below calmed. Instead of choppy waves, tranquil ripples danced on the surface.

"That's amazing, Coral," said Topaz. "As still and clear as a bath."

Coral curtsied.

Topaz could see all the way to the bottom.

"There it is," said Opal. "The treasure chest!"

A wooden chest with glinting golden fastenings nestled between the rocks.

"It's pretty deep, Topaz." said Pearl. "I don't know if you'll be able to hold your breath for long enough. I only managed because of my mermaid powers."

Jade looked up. "Use this!" she said. Jade thrust something into Topaz's hand. It was made from bits of metal—things Jade had found on the ship, Topaz guessed—and reeds from the side of the pool. It looked like a small flute—silver, with a mouthpiece on the side—but with a mesh of leaves at the end.

"What is this?" Topaz asked.

"It's a breathing device!" Jade smiled proudly. "I just saw how to make it in my head."

Topaz put the device to her mouth and sucked. "Are you sure it'll work?"

"Certain," Jade replied, chin in the air.

"Well there's only one way to find out," Topaz said, as she stepped to the edge of the waterfall. It was a massive jump, but she couldn't think about that now.

Deep breath...

Jade squeezed her eyes tight shut. "I can't watch," she whispered.

Topaz threw herself forward and dived—for the second time in ten minutes—into the pool far, far below. The water was still cold, but thanks to Coral, it was calm.

Pearl swam to meet her, swooshing her tail up and down as if she'd been born with it. She took Topaz's hand and pulled her further down— Jade's breathing device worked! Underwater, the pool was seemingly bottomless, its sides made from jagged gray and black rocks. Gradually they swam deeper, and Topaz could see the chest resting on a rocky ledge. Pearl towed her toward it.

The wood was cracked a bit in places—probably because of being wet for so long. But the gold clasp shone brightly. Topaz was desperate to see inside, but the clasp was locked shut. How would they get it open? And there was a bigger problem to tackle first—how would they get it out of the pool?

Topaz pushed her fingers under the chest as far as they'd go. Wiggling her arm under it, she picked the chest up from the rocky ledge. It was no harder than giving Pearl a piggyback at school. Pearl laughed, bubbles floating from her mouth and Topaz felt a rush of pride.

Topaz kicked for the surface, and Pearl grabbed on to her to help. It felt like swimming through peanut butter, but at last they broke through the water's surface.

Topaz

The Sunken Treasure

The other girls and Jasper had climbed down to the pool's edge. Opal was biting her fingernails.

"You made it!" said Coral.

"Well done," said Jasper.

"We did it together with the help of Jade's brilliant invention," said Topaz, dragging the heavy chest out of the pool. Pearl leaped out after her and as soon as her tail left the water, the scales shimmered and transformed back into legs. "This is the best!" said Pearl and the friends all giggled.

Topaz examined the chest closely. The lock was thick, but the keyhole was a very familiar shape. She put her ring in the lock and it clicked open instantly, as if it was brand new. Topaz took a deep breath—somehow this was much scarier than jumping off the waterfall—and opened the chest.

Inside the chest a big, beautiful, honey-colored gemstone glinted as water rushed out. It was the same color as the one in her ring—cut into a perfect cube.

"Topaz." Jasper whispered.

"Yup," said Topaz, unable to tear her eyes away from the gem.

"No, that's what the gem is—a topaz," said Jasper. "It's the Orange Isle's magical Treasure."

Topaz picked it up. It fitted snugly into the palm of her hand.

"Whoa," said Coral. "It's beautiful, Topaz. That stone belongs to your family...to you."

Topaz felt proud. But the Treasure didn't belong to her; it belonged to the island. If Jasper was right, it would restore the Orange Isle to the beautiful, exotic place she saw in her dreams.

"A cutlass!" said Pearl, reaching into the chest. She pulled out a curved golden sword. Vines were engraved on both the blade and the handle.

Suddenly, the cruel howls of the wolves echoed through the caves. They were closer now —much closer.

Topaz knew they didn't have much time, but she had to see what else was in the chest. She picked out a photograph. It was faded by water damage, but still visible were a couple—the man and woman from Topaz's dreams—holding a baby in their arms.

"That's you," said Jade.

The baby was obviously Topaz, from her dark, inquisitive eyes and olive skin, to the tufts of auburn hair on her head. Baby Topaz was wrapped in a purple cloth—Topaz's favorite color. She felt a lump in her throat. This was a picture of the parents she'd always longed to meet.

Another woman stood with the family. She

was dressed all in white, her hair flowing down to the floor. She seemed strangely familiar.

"That's Celestine the seawitch," Jasper told her.

"What's this?" said Coral. She picked up a scroll. "How come it's not been destroyed by the water?"

"Magic," said Pearl confidently.

Topaz unrolled the scroll, her heart pounding, scared of what she might find. It was a handwritten letter. Topaz held her breath as she read.

Beloved Topaz,

If you're reading this you have found your way back to Lemuria—your home.

We have loved you from the moment you were born. Our darling baby girl.

We're gone now, but that doesn't mean our

love for you has disappeared. We miss you and we're so, so proud of you.

The letter continued, but Topaz couldn't read any more. Tears were streaming down her face.

***

The friends ran the whole way along the riverbank, back to the throne room, hoping to beat Obsidian's henchmen. Topaz was still shaken by what she had seen and read, but they had a job to do.

"We must restore the Treasure into the crown," Jasper said.

"Where exactly *is* the crown?" Pearl asked.

Jasper screwed up his face. "I don't know..."

As Topaz looked at the map, a glowing crown symbol appeared. She sat on one of the thrones to examine the map more closely. The moment she sat, the gemstone disappeared from her hand. "Oh!" She cried, dropping the map.

"What in the oceans...?" gasped Opal.

Topaz felt something heavy on her head. She reached up and touched something cold and metal.

"The gemstone's on the front of it!" gasped Jade.

Topaz couldn't wait any longer. She reached up and removed a golden crown from her head. The large topaz stone shone out from the front of it.

Suddenly, there was a sound of running water. The fountains and waterfalls in the throne room began to trickle, then flow, pouring out water. More water gushed down the gully in the middle of the room, creating a pretty stream.

Cheers and cries of surprise came through the windows, and Topaz and her friends ran to see what was happening. The fountains outside were flowing too! Bare trees sprouted leaves and began to grow fruit. Plant shoots sprang up from the ground. People were gathering outside, laughing, clapping, even weeping with joy.

"The Treasure magic works!" said Opal.

"Everything is coming back to life!" said Jade.

"Topaz, you totally fixed the island!" said Pearl.

"*We* totally fixed the island," Topaz said, and she pulled her friends in for a hug.

"Take this, Topaz," said Coral, taking the cutlass they had found from Pearl. "It'll complete your look."

Topaz took the cutlass and slipped it into her belt. With this and the golden crown, she really felt like a princess. The savior the seawitch had promised the people.

Then she realized Jasper wasn't celebrating.

He was just behind them, staring, his eyes

full of tears. "I knew it was you," he said, his voice quiet.

"Jasper," said Coral. "Are you *crying*?"

Jasper turned away and shook his head. "No," he sniffed. "Hay fever."

Coral put her arm around him. "You big softie," she said. "How does it feel getting a hug from a princess pirate?"

"Princess pirate, princess pirate!" Pegleg squawked, flying in circles above them.

The celebrations abruptly ended when a shrill voice boomed from across the room. "Princesses!"

Topaz spun around to see a tall woman with a black cloak and a menacing scowl.

Obsidian.

"It *is* you," she growled.

Topaz stood with her chin raised, unafraid.

"I'll have that gemstone now," Obsidian

snarled.

"You wish, Obsidian!" Topaz replied.

Topaz took off the crown and stowed it in her top. It was more precious than anything. It was the link to her family and she wasn't going to give it up without a fight.

The Sunken Treasure

Chapter 10

Topaz glanced across to see Pearl standing beside her, hands on hips.

"Yeah," said Opal, stepping forward to join them. "You're not getting that stone."

"Good luck trying! My friends are the toughest princesses you'll ever meet," said Jade.

Topaz had to work hard to stop herself from smiling. She loved Jade referring to them as tough princesses, but even better was her calling them friends.

"I don't need luck," Obsidian spat. "Larry!

Boil!" The two men stepped out from the shadows behind her. Their wolves were straining at their leashes.

Topaz gulped as Larry and Boil released Snarl and Menace, who ran to within biting distance. The wolves snapped and growled, drool dripping from their tongues.

"Leave us alone," Opal pleaded with the animals. "Can't you see what Obsidian is doing is wrong?"

The wolves growled some more.

Opal shook her head. "They still say they have to obey their masters."

Topaz always had a plan, but right now, she didn't have a clue. "We can't let down the people of the island." she thought aloud.

"That's it," Opal whispered. "The people...and the *animals!*"

"You have two seconds to hand over that crown," said Obsidian, striding toward them.

"No way," said Topaz, still holding it close.

Snarl and Menace gnashed their teeth. Larry and Boil chuckled cruelly.

"Animals of the Orange Isle!" Opal shouted to the sky. "We need your help!"

Obsidian lowered her voice. "Kill them!"

Snarl and Menace stepped forward and bared their massive sharp teeth. Their sinister growls made Topaz's skin crawl.

Suddenly, a mass of white and gray flew in through the window—seagulls! They whooshed past Jasper and the girls, then swooped down to peck Snarl and Menace. Pegleg joined in too, biting both wolves—on the tail, on the legs,

on their necks. Snarl and Menace twisted and squealed trying to avoid them.

"Good work, Pegleg!" shouted Jasper.

A hiss made Topaz turn. It was a stray cat with matted ginger fur.

Larry laughed. "What does this mangy little cat think it can do against my wolves?"

Another cat appeared beside it. Then another. And another.

"Hello, friends," Opal said. The cats meowed back, then started to circle the wolves.

A scuttling, tapping sound, and movement along the floor made Topaz jump. Crabs! They came in their hundreds, pincers raised. They pinched the paws of the wolves, who cowered behind their masters.

"Don't be scared of a bunch of walking seashells—attack!" Larry ordered. A crab pinched his toe and he shrieked in pain.

A shadow at the back of the room caught Topaz's eye. There, in front of the waterfall, was a large stag with antlers that looked like small trees. The wolves took one look at the majestic beast and ran—tails between their legs. Larry and Boil followed.

"We'd better go too," said Topaz. "Back to Nestor!"

The girls ran to the grand entrance just in front of the stream that flowed through the middle of the room. But Obsidian stepped in front of them, blocking their path.

"Not so fast, little princesses," she said. Obsidian held out her staff. The black jewel at the end glinted menacingly.

"Move it, Obsidian," said Opal.

Obsidian's smile dropped and she stamped her staff down hard on to the stone floor. Sparks shot from the stone and the room shook, causing parts of the ceiling to crumble. Jasper and the girls covered their heads with their arms. Pegleg squawked and flapped in terror.

But Topaz lifted her chin. This was her island and she would protect it. Her parents had sent her away to safety so she could return and save Lemuria. She wasn't going to let them down. Topaz put the crown back on and stepped forward.

"Out of my way, witch," she said, feeling the weight of the cutlass at her side. She pulled it out and swiped at Obsidian, but Obsidian dodged. Topaz swiped again, knocking the staff out of Obsidian's hand and into the stream that ran through the throne room.

"Noooooo!" Obsidian cried. She jumped into the stream, drenching her clothes and hair, and thrashed about, searching for her staff.

"Let's not hang around," said Jade, grabbing

Topaz's arm.

"That is not a good look," Coral said with a giggle as she raced out of the door. Topaz ran out too.

"I'll get you, you stinking princesses!" shrieked Obsidian, as the friends hurried down the grand stone steps at the front of the palace.

"We did it!" cried Pearl. "We got the gemstone and beat Obsidian, too!"

"That's what I call a good day's work!" said Opal.

The town was so different from how it had

looked earlier. Green plants grew everywhere. Climbing flowers curled around posts and columns, releasing a beautiful exotic scent. A little boy tucked into a juicy mango, waving at them as they passed.

"The princesses!" he cried. "You did it!"

Topaz grinned back. Together, the princess friends had done so much.

The girls soon reached Nestor, panting from their run. Barney the shipwright was sitting dangling from a rope off the side of the ship, hammer and nails in hand. The hole from the cannonball was patched with shiny new planks of wood.

"How's he doing?" Jasper asked Barney.

Barney scratched his beard. "Patched up right nice for an old ship," he replied.

"Oi!" Nestor called from the front. "I'm old, but I'm not deaf!"

Topaz bit her lip to stop herself laughing. Nestor looked as regal as ever, his mane carved to look like he was traveling at speed. Seeing him was like seeing a favorite old uncle.

"I'm glad you're OK, Nestor," she told him.

"I knew you could do it," he said. "Your parents would be so proud."

Instantly, a lump rose in Topaz's throat. She was just able to choke out a *thank you* before running up the gangplank and onto the main deck.

"All friends on deck?" she called to her crew.

"Aye aye, Captain!" they called back.

Barney tipped his cap and jumped off his seat. But Coral grabbed him and hugged him before he could go. "Thanks, Barney."

Barney blushed bright red—even through his sunburn! He gave a hurried half-bow. "You're welcome, your highnesses."

Topaz stood by the wheel and gave the command to hoist the sails. Before long, they were out of the harbor and back on the high seas. The palace on the Orange Isle was where she was born. Breakwater Hall was where she had grown up. But here on the water, thought Topaz, with the wind rushing around her and waves crashing against the bow, was where she felt at home.

"Where to?" asked Jasper, unfurling the magical map. Pegleg was on his shoulder, happily eating a peanut.

Topaz saw the different islands—*The White Isle, The Orange Isle, The Green Isle, The Purple Isle, The Pink Isle, The Island of the Five Thrones.*

"Which island is whose?" asked Pearl.

"Let mine be the Pink Isle," Coral said to herself, fingers crossed.

"I hope mine is this one," said Opal, pointing

out the purple-flowered plains of the Purple Isle. "Can we go there next?"

"I want to swim like a mermaid again," said Pearl.

"We need to visit all the islands and make sure all the gemstones are safe," said Jade.

"And we need to rescue Jasper's parents," added Topaz.

Jasper smiled gratefully, his eyes filling a little.

Topaz wanted nothing more than to stay in Lemuria and help the people and animals of the amazing world she came from, but there was one thought worrying her. "We need to keep this gemstone from Obsidian."

The girls nodded.

"So where do we hide it?" asked Pearl.

"Bury it?" suggested Coral.

"There's only one place she'll never find it,"

said Topaz.

The girls nodded again. They lived in a different world, which only they could get to. It was the safest place of all.

"We have to take it back to Breakwater Hall," Jade said.

"You're leaving?" said Jasper, as he pushed his hands into his messy brown hair. "But what about Lemuria? Obsidian is angrier than ever."

"We'll be back," Topaz promised him. "We just need to hide the gem first."

Jasper opened his mouth to protest, but then changed his mind. "You're right," he said. "But you'll return? Promise?"

"Princess promise!" said Pearl, holding out her little finger. Jasper wrapped his little finger around hers and said goodbye, before he set off back to shore in a little rowing boat, Pegleg perched on his shoulder.

"I like him," said Coral.

All the girls turned to look at her, eyebrows raised.

Coral blushed. "Not like *that!*"

The others laughed. "We'll see him again," said Opal.

Topaz nodded. "Just as soon as we hide the gem safely at school."

"Errrr...how do we get back to school?" asked Pearl.

Topaz thought hard. Jasper had taken the map, but Topaz didn't remember any signs of how to travel to their world on it.

"Same way you got here!" Nestor called out.

Topaz thought back to how their adventure had begun. Jade had fallen into the lake and they'd saved her. They'd pulled her out together and...

"That's it!" Topaz cried. "Ring bump!"

She put her fist out and the others did the same.

"Here goes," said Topaz.

"See you soon, Lemuria," said Coral.

And they touched their rings together.

Instantly, there was a flash of golden light and Topaz squeezed her eyes shut. When she opened them, she was in her purple  pajamas, in their little boat, gently bobbing up and down on Lapis Lake. It was the dead of night, but the water was calm and the moon was bright, and she could see Breakwater Hall on the shore. Despite everything, it was good to be back.

"Nestor?" Opal whispered.

But there was no reply.

"He's finally stopped yelling at us!" said Jade. The other girls laughed.

"So what do you think about sailing now, Jade?" Topaz asked her, putting an arm around her. "Want to learn?"

Jade cringed. "I think I'd better, don't you?"

Topaz pointed to the jib rope. "Lesson one: pull that, slowly and steadily."

Jade did as Topaz said. Soon the sail caught the light breeze and they headed back to the dock. They tied Nestor up and put everything away, as if their adventure had never happened.

Creeping back into Breakwater Hall the way they left it—up the zigzagging stairs, through the gate, through the herb garden, and into the building—they stayed silent...until they passed the grandfather clock in the hall.

"It says it's 1:25," whispered Opal. "Do you

think we've been gone a whole day and night?"

"Miss Whitestone will be really worried," Pearl whispered back.

Topaz saw a sock on the floor—the same one they'd passed as they walked down the stairs. She shook her head. "I don't think any time has passed at all!"

More magic!

"Girls!" came a voice from above them. Miss Whitestone! She was in a white dressing gown, her white hair in a hairnet. "What are you doing down here?"

Topaz swallowed hard. "We were..."

"We were thirsty?" said Opal.

"All of you?" Miss Whitestone narrowed her violet eyes. "At the same time?"

"Umm..." said Opal. None of them could answer that one.

Miss Whitestone sighed heavily as she

walked toward them. "You need to be careful if you sneak out at night," she said. "Who knows where you'll wash up?"

Topaz frowned. That was a strange thing to say! And Miss Whitestone didn't even sound that cross. Maybe she was still half-asleep.

"Yes, Miss Whitestone," said Jade.

"Sorry, Miss Whitestone," said Coral.

"We'll get to bed now, Miss Whitestone," said Opal.

The others scurried up the stairs and Topaz started to follow them.

"Topaz," Miss Whitestone called.

Topaz winced. The others stopped dead, just in front of her. She turned slowly to face her head teacher.

"Yes, Miss Whitestone?" she said.

"That's not school uniform." She pointed at Topaz's head.

Topaz reached up. The crown! It was still there!

She couldn't help smiling. At least now she knew the adventure was definitely real. She took off the crown, cradling it in her arms.

"I can explain. You see…" But Topaz couldn't explain at all.

"Jewelry is not allowed in school, as you well know," Miss Whitestone said, her lips pursed. "Put it somewhere safe. We'd hate it to fall into the wrong hands, wouldn't we?"

Topaz's mouth fell open. She was wearing a golden crown with a gemstone and all Miss Whitestone could say was to hide it safely—just what Topaz intended! Suddenly she felt four pairs of hands on her arms.

"Come on, Topaz," her friends whispered, as they pulled her up the stairs.

Amazingly it seemed they were getting away

without a telling off so they hurried through the hallways and back to the dorm.

"Do you think Miss Whitestone knows where we've been?" asked Pearl.

"No," said Topaz, "she couldn't. *Could she?*"

Topaz pushed open the door to their dorm room. Her body ached with tiredness, but as she got into bed and turned off the lights her mind was still whirring.

"I can't believe we're princesses!" Coral squeaked.

They all giggled nervously.

"I don't really feel like a princess, though," said Topaz. She knew her parents had been the king and queen, but still...*princess* didn't feel quite right. "But a *pirate*," she thought aloud. "That's a title I can believe."

"We're princess pirates!" said Jade.

Topaz smiled. *Princess pirates*—that fits

nicely. They had defeated Obsidian once. And with her four best friends working as a team, they'd go back to Lemuria and defeat her again.

She couldn't wait for another princess pirates adventure.

TO BE CONTINUED...

Jade

The Clockwork City

Jade is super smart, but she will need help
from her friends to avoid the dangerous
traps that are waiting for her.

Can Jade find her way through the maze and
save the animals and people of the Green Isle?

Prepare to set sail with the Princess Pirates!

Book 2

ISBN: 978-1-78700-460-3